The Invisible Hand

Nathan Leslie

The Invisible Hand

Nathan Leslie

Hamilton Stone Editions
Maplewood, New Jersey

Library of Congress Cataloging-in-Publication Data
Title: The invisible hand / by Nathan Leslie.
Other titles: Invisible hand (Compilation)
Description: Maplewood, NJ : Hamilton Stone Editions, [2022] | Identifiers: LCCN 2022024786
ISBN 9781736500118 (trade paperback)
Subjects: LCGFT: Short stories.
Classification: LCC PS3612.E78 I58 2022 | DDC 813/.6--dc23/eng/20220629
LC record available at https://lccn.loc.gov/2022024786

First Edition

The short stories within this collection are works of fiction and any resemblance to living or deceased individuals is accidental.

H/S Hamilton Stone Editions
P.O. Box 43, Maplewood, New Jersey 07040

Special thanks to Lou Robinson and
Meredith Sue Willis

Also by Nathan Leslie:

As Editor:

Table of Contents

Baby Carrots in
Two Hundred and Forty-Four

1. We can't have children—"we" meaning "me."

2. My wife could likely have a child—many children—with another man, a more reproductively competent man.

3. Unfortunately, I'm not this man; I have flawed sperm. Defective swimmies. A maladjusted production line.

4. There is a medical term for this.

5. The medical term, however, is not frankly that important. What is important is the net effect of oligospermia.

6. The net effect of oligospermia is multifaceted.

7. If the net effect of oligospermia were a color it might be puce, perhaps a particularly pukey puce.

8. Or grey.

9. I'm struggling, frankly, with the cause and effect.

10. It is difficult to quantify.

11. It is difficult to be precise about these things.

12. A plus B=?

13. Activities I do more of than I used to (pre-diagnosis):

--Swill cabernet.

--Smoke cigarillos.

--Give the finger to motorists who act in a rude manner.

--Punch my pillow in frustration.

--Cry and wail.

--Swill vodka and Coke.

--Listen to the music of my youth: The Clash, etcetera, etcetera.

14. Activities which I rarely do compared to my previous (pre-diagnosis) existence:

--Tend to our rose bushes.

--Purchase peaches from the farmer's market.

--Listen to Miles Davis.

--Play softball for my church league.

--Make love to Celia, gently.

--Enjoy candlelight dinners.

--Research home repairs.

15. Last week my wife and I were out to eat at a tapas place—great food.

16. We sat at a table smack in the middle of the restaurant (I had asked for a private booth, but this was all they had available).

17. I felt uncomfortable, as if the entire restaurant was inspecting us—me in particular.

18. It was almost a physical sensation—I felt itchy in the eye holes.

19. "What?" I said to a man two tables over. "What?"

20. He looked off in the middle distance and failed to respond, or perhaps he didn't hear me.

21. "It's okay, Peter," Celia said. "It will be fine—please don't worry."

22. I felt she was being a Pollyanna, so I told her so. "You're being…"

23. The way in which I deal with emotions is to have them, confront them, move on.

24. My philosophy exactly, when I told her I feel like a useless piece of shit.

25. King Henry the Eighth decapitated his wives for their failure to produce an heir.

26. "So you want to have me decapitated, Peter?"

27. "Of course not. That's not what I'm saying. If anything…me, if anything."

28. "It's not as if….I mean, my womb--"

29. "Are you trying to make me feel better or worse?"

30. She drank her pinot grigio, bowed her head into the menus.

31. Good, I thought—tapas. Tapas.

32. "What're we getting?"

33. "Tapas," I said. "Some tapas, since we are here at the tapas restaurant here to eat some tapas."

34. We selected—rather I let her select.

35. Even if delicious, tapas is overpriced bullshit anyway—not a real meal; just an excuse to rake in money for over-priced appetizers.

36. Candles, soft Andres Segoviaesque plucking, warm atmospherics. Fine.

37. Lots of red, orange, yellow. Pandering?

38. We're supposed to think Spain—we're in Spain. Ole.

39. I'm thinking pedagogical strategies —bright colors to distract us, to keep us compliant, pliant.

40. Are we here for the food or the faux travel experience? I wonder.
41. No, we're there so we can tell our friends we had tapas last night.

42. So they'll be impressed (they'll know tapas ain't cheap), and they'll think more highly of us.

43. It's like marking territory with our feces—except that would be considerably less expensive.

44. We ate our marinated mussels.

45. We ate our white asparagus with yogurt and black olives.

46. We ate our chorizo wrapped in potato, our fennel salad with apples, our chicken croquetas.

47. "What? What? What?"

48. I'm evil-eyeing the couple with toddler; I'm evil-eying the couple with high school age daughter; I'm evil-eying the pregnant woman who sighs in my direction.

49. The fuckers don't know how lucky they have it.

50. Commandment number four squared. Do not envy thy neighbor's ability to reproduce their dumbshit genes.

51. Do not.

52. That night I sleep in the guest room.

53. The guest room is a might clammy—it's in the basement.

54. I don't care.

55. I wanted to keep my wife from seeing me at my worst.

56. She has a long way to go.

57. She descended to bring me to bed anyway.

58. I should've locked the door, but I didn't.

59. I wasn't asleep.

60. She curled up next to me—in the guest room.

61. We are guests in our own house, I thought.

62. We slept like that.

63. Celia whispered that "she doesn't want anything dividing us."

64. "It doesn't have to be something to worry over," she said.

65. "But it is," I said.

66. "You're so stubborn," she said.

67. She had me there.

68. I listened to her breathing—the movement of her lungs.

69. This calmed me—it did.

70. This was also the night the dreams began.

71. The dreams were vivid, initially colors—dreams of colors.

72. When you close your eyes you see a muted blackness.

73. In these dreams I saw a vivid puceness.

74. The dreams were more color than substance.

75. The color was the dreams: the puce blanketed the horses trampling over the desert floor, galloping into the distance to the sea where they would find a schooner and board it and sail for fifty days to an island of horses where they would congregate, breed, and through the process of evolution develop into a society, a civilization, an empire of horses—all this was puce.

76. And the puce horses swam to other islands and built schooners of their own and seeded the planet with their horseness, their puce horseness.

77. And they encountered humans, but the humans were little match for the immensity of the horses—these former beasts of burden.

78. I awoke in a sweat, wondering if I had ever abused a horse, ridden a horse, used a horse as a beast of burden.

79. There was a petting zoo—I may have abused a horse then, I thought.

80. I may have teased a horse, or more likely a pony.

81. Perhaps I didn't offer enough in the way of apple slices and sugar cubes and such.

82. Puce.

83. I began to see puce everywhere—in clothes, in cars, in rug patterns, in jewelry, in sandwiches, in the fur of cats, in upholstery, in the freckles of children, in bathroom wallpaper, in tree leaves, in weedy garden plots.

84. In paintings.

85. I went to an art gallery—Celia was at work and stared at the puce paintings: dead sparrows, olive trees, female peacocks.

86. The owner asked if she "could help me."

87. "You already are," I told her.

88. "Oh," she said. "How so?"

89. "The pallet; I dream in puce," I said.

90. Silence. Silence.

91. "The same color as your paintings," I said.

92. Silence.

93. "Do these paintings seem dreamlike to you?"

94. "No, you don't understand."

95. "They strike me as a latent attempt at representation, a post-modern, post-hierarchy—"

96. "They are my dreams," I said.

97. Which was true.

98. The more I saw, the more I realized what I saw was merely a reflection of what my mind unspooled in my unconscious.

99. I told her this.

100. She seemed nice, sweet, a young girl who just matriculated from her M.F.A. program.

101. She had a tattoo of a moon crescent on her wrist.

102. The moon almost looked watery, shimmering.

103. It was not puce.

104. The gallery girl:

--Henna hair.

--Pierced nose—silver stud.

--White t-shirt featured an upside down pink blue jay, who was also smoking a cigarette.

--Skin the color of concrete.

--Sandal thingies.

--Breasts compressed/squashed under her t-shirt.

--Crooked mouth.

--Slightly crossed eyes.

105. "What's the significance of the bird?"

106. "The bird?"

107. "On your shirt," I said.

108. "Oh," she said. "This. Something I got at this, you know, totally random thrift store."

109. I wondered if I would dream of pink blue jays, and if I did what kind of society they would form.

110. "I'm just going to stand here for a while," I said.

111. "Be my guest," she said.

112. So that's what I did, though she looked doubtful.

113. This is the only way to tell this story.

114. Otherwise it doesn't work, doesn't congeal.

115. This list is the ultimate congealer.

116. When Time Magazine doesn't know what to do, it makes a list.

117. We all make lists, different types of lists.

118. The list gives us a sense of purpose—a beginning, middle, end.

119. It ranks.

120. It provides a hierarchy in a hierarchy-less world.

121. Order.

122. She gave me that look.

123. That look is usually a result of judgment—something odd or unusual or bizarre which I did, and which the looker makes readily apparent.

124. This is problematic for them—not for me.

125. The judger is at fault, not the judged.

126. She gave me that look because I told her my sperm is defective, in those words, more or less.

127. Roughly that.

128. She picked up the phone to call. And then she called.

129. "Hello, security?"

130. I understood her concerns.

131. She could've been more compassionate, however.

132. Not to judge, but she could've listened to my story, my deep inner pain.

133. I told her this.

134. "I've asked you to leave," she said.

135. "You have?"

136. "Don't play dub—at any rate, security is on its way."

137. So I left—fine.

138. Who needs the hassle of strangers?

139. Who needs the waste of time?

140. As if security scares me.

141. Rent-a-cops.

142. Rent-a-jerks.

143. Celia was a good woman, still is.

144. Celia has been responsible enough to pay the bills and tend to the domestics and work part-time as a barista at Stonehenge Coffee on top of her position as

an employee of the U.S. of A—meaning the Feds, the gov, the man.

145. She is the man.

146. She likes the stability, the comfort it gives her on a daily basis.

147. She feels as if the position she has can't easily be liquidated or eliminated.

148. She feels as if she's solid.

149. I think every time you're solid you're not really solid.

150. That's usually the moment solidity transforms to liquidity.

151. E.g., my defective swimmies.

152. Really….

153. So she was not present when I returned home.

154. Celia was out earning the bacon, while I doodled and dabbled.

155. I took a long nap.

156. When I awoke from said long nap I could hear sounds emanate from the kitchen, sounds of food preparation, clinking and clanking.

157. I made my way—no hurry—to the kitchen to find her unloading the dishwasher, sliding plates into the cupboard.

158. I realized that I hadn't done this activity in quite a long time.

159. Years. Many years.

160. I sat at the kitchen table in front of her.

161. She burned a scented candle—smelled of vanilla bean.

162. Enya on the speakers.

163. She unwinds in this way. Everyone has their own flawed methods.

164. Then it hit me.

165. The dream of the baby carrots.

166. In my dream baby carrots hung in space, like a mobile. Rotating above an infant's crib.

167. They were smooth and an orange color unknown to me—an almost fluorescent orange, the orange of the brightest nubile sun.

168. These baby carrots seemed laden with…something. Spirit; substance; personality.

169. They were there, floating.

170. I wanted to tell her; even more than that, I wanted to return to the baby carrots, to the dream.
171. I wasn't sure what to say.

172. **Paralysis.**

173. "What would you like for dinner?" she asked.

174. It was an innocent enough question.

175. I wanted to tell her baby carrots, carrot soup perhaps, carrot cake.

176. And yet…something about the baby carrots.

177. "I don't feel well," I told her.

178. "Oh, I'm sorry."

179. "I think I need to go back to bed," I told her.

180. In the guest room.

181. Away from her, from everything that is.

182. The glimpse had given me a hunger for more.

183. I traveled.

184. I didn't like to travel, but I did: train then bus then taxi then one foot in front of another.

185. Mr. Brig was tall and bald and came equipped with a hunched, shuffling walk.

186. He was the "foreman"—at least this is what his shirt clip thingie said.

187. He seemed to be the kind of man who didn't suffer fools easily.

188. I wonder if I was a fool to him.

189. In retrospect I must have seemed to be one.

190. He was not the nice lady who corresponded with me via e-mail, telling me that Farmer's United Baby Carrot Factory would "simply love to offer me a tour of the facility."

191. I told her I had to find the source.

192. "I'm not sure what you mean by 'source,'" she responded.

193. "Source of the baby carrots. I have to find out how they are born."

194. Mr. Brig was not the nice lady, but he did wear a paisley tie, which was green and gold and red.

195. If they were orange, the dollops would perhaps have reminded me of baby carrots.

196. His face was pitted.

197. I watched the pits squinch and unsquinch as he spoke to me, as he showed me.

198. "This is the line," he said, speaking almost delicately.

199. "I mean assembly line—we call it 'the line.'"

200. I wonder if he spoke softly so that he didn't wake the baby carrots.

201. "This is where it begins," he said, pointing to a machine which was peeling carrots.

202. They were long, fairly large carrots.

203. I asked him where the baby carrots were.

204. "These will be baby carrots in a few minutes," he said.

205. "We start with regular carrots."

206. "I thought….I thought."

207. "They aren't miniature carrots. They are abbreviated carrots."

208. "I thought…."

209. "They are regular carrots which are peeled and processed; that's what a baby carrot is."

210. I didn't know what to say.

211. I listened, but inside I was sighing.

212. He showed me the stair step conveyor belt.

213. The small peeled carrots rise up, rise up, rise up.

214. They were suddenly baby carrots.

215. He showed me another conveyor belt where the baby carrots are pushed along and dried.

216. He showed me another conveyor belt where ladies with large orange gloves made swooping motions with their hands to pick out any impure baby carrots.

217. I thought it was odd that the ladies wore orange gloves.

218. I wondered who made that decision.

219. Didn't the orange of the baby carrots blend with the orange of the gloves?

220. I mean, didn't the ladies have trouble discerning which orange was which? They could have chosen a cleaner color variation.

221. Mr. Brig cleared his throat, a lot.

222. I believe he was attempting to tell me not to stare, but I was in a tour so why not?
223. Perhaps he was attempting to tell me to move on.

224. Perhaps he wasn't attempting to tell me much of anything at all and something just stuck in his throat.

225. However, he didn't seem to be that kind of guy to me.

226. We watched the baby carrots swoosh down and swoop up and packaged in a frenzy.

227. I watched them tumble by the hundreds, thousands.

228. I watched them slide and skid.

229. For some reason, I stopped thinking of procreation.

230. I was transfixed by the rolling, orange, wet **vegetables.**

231. "Can I..."

232. "Sample?"

233. "Uh, yes," I said.

234. "Right this way," Mr. Brig said, flicking his finger forward.

235. There was a room and in this room were hundreds upon hundreds of baby carrots with all kinds of vegetable dip.

236. I took one and dipped it into the white dressing and it snapped in my mouth ever-so-nicely.

237. I could feel the head of the baby carrot crunch in my mouth and it felt and tasted good.

238. I was eating it and swallowing this little guy.
239. My pain.

240. "I love you," I said, grabbing the next baby carrot.

241. A reedy looking woman with long brown hair stared at me. Into me.

242. I wanted to tell her, "That's right—I'm talking to the baby carrot and then I'm eating it."

243. Eat the conundrum, I thought.

244. Eat it good.

The Invisible Hand

1.

Is there a story? An obituary doesn't tell the story of a life—it provides a portrait. Tell a portrait—that should be my goal.

Long before we met, I followed my father. I was a young, inquisitive guy. Eighteen or Nineteen. I was sort of a passive skeptic who silently questioned everything around me. I failed to verbalize my questioning; I took note.

The weekend days on which my father vanished— they multiplied. He would drive off in the morning glare, sunglasses on—a cooler of food occupying the front seat. He never told us where he was headed. "Just out for a drive," he'd say with a tone of even neutrality. The fact that he'd return eight hours later, however, gave me pause. I had heard of polygamists, of men with other, secret wives. Other families. I suspected the worst.

"Don't you wonder?" I asked my mother.

This was the beginning of her illness; in retrospect I wonder if he knew.

"It's not my business, Frankie," she'd say. She'd embrace me, then pull back and pat my shoulders. "The bureau needs dusting."

She'd spend all day Saturday—every Saturday— cleaning. It was her therapy. This, for some reason, rent my heart in two. I thought of her as a martyr. I thought of my father as an overlord.

I made my decision.

2.

Arthur Sutton Lowe was in insurance. He insured others, assured them, also. I somehow grew up thinking of my father's job as his chosen religion. What he did he was. However, even as a young child, I was deeply uninterested in the day-to-day happenings at the office. Come dinner time, my father would occasionally discuss the performance of this or that insurance salesman, or recount the damage done by a certain fire or the ins-and-outs of a car accident.

Fires, car accidents, robbery—I should have been captivated by the bird's eye view my father provided for us. Yet, this was not so. Primarily, this was not so because my father spoke softly, in a kind of hushed mumble. Also, he frequently told his stories out of sequence; they were a hash.

As I matured into my teenage years, my father eventually ceased discussing work altogether. Perhaps my mother sensed my lack of interest; perhaps my father had simply given us all the angles we needed on his life at the office; perhaps he simply shared the intimate details later with my mother. At any rate, when my mother asked him how his day went, his answer would invariably go: "not bad."

Later in the evening my father would turn the baseball game on low and read a biography. He was fascinated by the intimate details of famous strangers— Napoleon, Tolstoy, Charles the Fifth, Einstein. Nursing a rum and water, he'd sit in his green upholstered armchair, reading and casually watching the game out of the corner of his eye.

By eleven I'd see the book splayed face-down on the floor, and my father would—empty glass in hand— be fast asleep. My mother would flip the lamp off, withdraw the glass from his hand, and lead him to bed.

I would remain, flipping the television from channel to channel rapidly until my mother told me I had school in the morning. I can still smell the worn fibers of that rug.

3.

My father—if you must know—was what many would consider a handsome man. He simply had little, if any, awareness of this brute fact. His defining trait: he wore large rimless glasses, as if the glass ovals floated invisibly on his face. The scraggly map of his curly hair was exacerbated by his mangy sideburns. He wore lime-green suits, chocolate brown blazers, clunky shoes which he likely purchased from Goodwill. My father also wore heavy, musk-based cologne. I recall my mother telling him one day that married men don't usually wear such things.

"The purpose of cologne," she said, laughing, "is to use that musky secretive scent to attract a mate. This is the purpose of musk. You already *have* me. What do you need cologne for?"

My father's insistence helped lead to my suspicions.

4.

The day I followed my father was breezy and cool—one of those mid-May dream days, yet cooler than you'd expect. In the 60's. The sky was clear. The sun dazzled. The tree boughs overhead oscillated back and forth.

I hovered five or six cars back, hoping to cloak myself.

He drove and drove. He took the highway west into the mountains. The traffic thinned and the horizon opened ahead of us. I had to lurk half a mile back so he didn't see me.

I listened to Chopin's piano sonatas. I'm not usually inclined to classical music, but I wanted something hushed to calm my pulsing heart.

5.

My father's father called it "the invisible hand." I think he confused the concept with Adam Smith's but his conflation stuck with me.

"You should always lead with an invisible hand," he said. I can still picture him leaning over the fire as he said this, prodding the embers. "You don't need to say much to be a leader," he said. "You just do what you do and the followers will fall in line behind. That's the way it works."

Then he sat in his maroon La-Z-Boy. I sat on the floor eyeballing the sparks. My father sat in the other armchair, hands clasped politely at his waist. We stayed like this for a long time. My father drank a mug of hot water. The steam clouded his glasses.

"How's your car running?"

"It's good," I said. "It's fine."

The wood burned hot and crackled.

"Never let other people dictate your life for you," he said. "Call the shots when you have them. Every time." He jabbed at the air with his forefinger.

6.

My father was duty bound. Any time a funeral arose, he was there. If a neighbor needed a hand, he had one to lend. In many respects, he was a man from another era. Though he was just a boy in the 1950's, it marked him.

In my youth we spent many days on the baseball field. He drove me back and forth, to and fro. He would stay and watch, but always from the car. I'd see him waving to me from behind the steering wheel. It was unnerving—as if at any moment he might decide to take off.

Parents volunteered to bring snacks for the players. They rotated. When my father's turn came up he brought a bag of ice. The boys looked at the bag quizzically.

"Is there something in the ice?" one of my teammates finally asked. "Or what?"

"Just frozen water," my father said. "Which is what ice is."

"Oh," the boy said.

A few chomped on squares ice out of politeness.

"Mmm, nice and cold," one boy said. "Good ice."

7.

When mom died, he seemed hesitant to reminisce. Our neighbors would arrive armed with pies and brownies and casseroles and offers to provide "a helping hand." "She was such a good person," the proclaimed. He cut them off, thanked them for their attention. My father looked forward. For this reason he rarely if ever took photographs. Odd, I know.

"I store it up here," he said.

He didn't seem to wallow deep in mourning, but then it was so difficult to ever tell what he thought or felt.

The only noticeable change my father made was that he became an active gardener. Growing up, looming oaks and maples flanked my parents' house. Where other neighbors cut down the trees, my parents liked the cool shade, the lowered electric bill in the summer. However, the yard frequently looked scraggly—moss and dirt; grass didn't grow.

A few months after my mother died, my father bought landscaping stones and a bevy of hostas. He positioned the stones around the yard in beautiful clusters and planted around them. He purchased a lawn bench, shade flowers, a small koi pond. I imagined sometimes—knowing my father was not a man of great sentimentality—that the bond was dedicated to my mother, affixed with a plaque in back. However, my father never went this far. He never did.

8.

He turned onto a side road. I saw a brown state park sign. I had to stay back lest he spot me. I followed him down the forest road through patches of sun and shadow. In places crows hunkered along the shoulder.

My father entered the state park entrance. I pulled off onto the shoulder so that I could swoop in, catch him unawares. I imagined a melodramatic scene—my father with another woman in his arms, my poor, sick mother at home biding her time until her unfaithful husband deigned to show his face again.

I waited five minutes. Everything pulsated. At the end of five minutes I counted to one hundred, took a deep breath and pulled my car into the park entrance.

9.

My father retired several years ago—to North Dakota of all places. He lived for a while in a small double-wide in a small town, waiting for the construction company to build his home. "The problem is," he told me on the phone. "There just aren't that many people out here."

Many men would complain of the cold and desolation. My father *chose* this desolation. Something about him.

I told my father I'd visit him once the house was finished. I haven't yet.

I imagine my father in four layers of clothes, watching game shows on a crackling television with bad reception. Drinking whiskey from a smudged glass. This, I think, is a misconception. Still, what does one do out in North Dakota, two thousand miles from his family? He's an island.

10.

I would say "friends and family" if my father had friends. He never did. He invested his time and energy in (1) his wife (2) me and (3) his work. End of story.

"Friends," he used to say. "Are fine. They just don't keep you warm at night."

11.

I drove around the loopy park entrance looking for my father's green station wagon. After making a complete circuit I didn't see him anywhere—not parked in front of any of the cabins, not parked in front of a hiking trail. I was at a loss. But I decided to circle back one more time. I had driven all this way and I didn't want to simply give up or give in. I thought perhaps he had driven down some hidden driveway only he knew about—his rendezvous.

On my second circuit, I suddenly saw his station wagon off to the left tucked back behind some picnic benches; I must have completely overlooked it. When I pulled into the parking lot he turned and saw me. He was sitting on a rock watching the creek. Alone. He was by himself.

I didn't know what to do, so I stopped the car and let it idle. He looked at me over his shoulder (this pose will be forever emblazoned in my mind) and then he turned back. My father sat there watching the creek. He was alone.

I never asked him about the park; I was too ashamed. I knew I had somehow let him down. My mother later, before she died—told me he had never been unfaithful to her. I believe her now.

12.

What is the story? Is there a story? I don't know. I'm telling you all this in hopes you'll understand. As you know, he won't be there when we walk down the aisle. He won't send his regards. My father is just a different kind of person.

He's not a bad man. He is built in a certain way for unknowable reasons—and really I can't possibly begin to speculate. But he lived his life the way he wanted, I suppose. Breath to breath.

Someday you can accompany me out there to meet him. You'll clasp my hand and you'll be nervous. He doesn't ask about me; he won't ask about you. He's growing deaf in one ear regardless. He'll be taciturn and he will seem steely and foreboding. We'll acclimate. We're in this together, from tomorrow on.

A Modern Parable

The father was an ungenerous man. He scrimped on gifts. He avoided thanking others. If invited to a dinner party, he would arrive empty-handed. He saw no earthly reason to abide by societal niceties. These, he felt, were for other, less rigorous people.

His face was slender, almost gaunt—skin pulled drum-tight over his cheek bones. His skin was reddish in hue and it flushed easily upon the slightest remark. His ears lay flat against his skull, and his fine nose gave him a fragile appearance. The father kept his hair cropped close. His eyes were small and quick in darting movement.

Despite his unintimidating presence, he was intense and opinionated. In an argument he'd often shout down his opponent—defeating them with sheer conviction and brawn.

The father married young—when he was twenty-two. His logic was simple—efficiency. The father saw no reason to "play the field" when he was well-acquainted with a perfectly fine woman. His wife was beautiful and delicate and passive and she bore him two sons. Nothing could have pleased the father more. After the birth of the second, the father insisted she get "that operation." Two is plenty, he said. "One more than the Chinese are allowed."

The father clearly preferred Son 1 to Son 2. He made no secret of this. The father was not of the belief that one must hide one's innermost thoughts and feelings to "protect the children." He believed, instead, that it would be dishonest to lie to them. Honesty was more important. He often referred to Son 1 as "my heir" and Son 2 as "you, kid."

Son 1 grew up to be a stout bully of a boy. He was broad-shouldered and strong, quick tempered and forceful with his opinions. Son 1 excelled at athletics, which garnered him social status and acclaim. Son 1 walked with an obvious strut that announced his perceived self-importance. He often did impromptu pushups or jumping jacks. "Just to stay fit," he said. His teachers cut him a wide berth.

Son 2 grew up to be a meek boy—thin, pale and knob-kneed, Son 2 was often a male wallflower. He shrunk from the spotlight, didn't seem to like the attention. His mother said he was shy, but Son 2 seemed, by his very posture, to accept his inferior status. His shoulders slumped. He hung his head. Son 2 often gazed at his feet or off into the distance. His handshake was cold and limp.

The two boys did not, in fact, fight often. The pecking order was clear and Son 2 saw little advantage to the idea of challenging it. The deck was so stacked, Son 2 thought any kind of uprising would only hurt him in the long run. However, when the boys *did* fight it was brutal. Son 1 would beat Son 2 in the face with a plastic bat or stick. "I'm going to bash your stupid head in," Son 1 would say. "Crush you." The mother would take Son 2 to the hospital, cushioning his bleeding face in her lap, patting his hair down.

"What happened, darling?" the mother would ask. "I am so sorry."

"I ate his pickle," Son 2 would say.

The father attended Son 1's athletic competitions—football and wrestling and soccer and boxing. He built shelves to house Son 1's trophies and awards. He took the family out to celebrate Son 1's latest glories. His birthday and Christmas presents were lavish—BMX bikes and stereo systems and cars and nights with expensive female escorts.

The father told Son 2 that unless he "found himself," Son 1 would reap the entirety of his attentions. "You don't have a whole lot going on," he told Son 2. Otherwise the father ignored Son 2 altogether, wrote him off. He told the mother that Son 2 was "hers." She said she loved both boys equally, but the father shrugged it off. "That's you," he said. "Not me."

As a grown man, Son 1 became an investment banker—a high-roller. On the side, he found a way to box and lift weights and wrestle. He maintained multiple simultaneous girlfriends, resigned to their status as one-of-several. He drove expensive cars, drank martinis, vacationed in far-flung tropical islands.

Son 2 became a first grade teacher—showing young children how to paste googly eyes to construction paper and add eight to five. Son 2 became close to his mother. He would visit her and they'd play cards and drink white wine and listen to Mendelssohn. If his father came into the room they'd exchange tense pleasantries until it became too uncomfortable.

The father would go on outings with Son 1—Vegas or Reno or Atlantic City. They would gamble and drink and hire hookers and take turns with them. Afterward they'd smoke cigars together on the hotel balcony and look over the glittering excess. "Man, oh man," the father would say.

One day Son 1 had a few too many shots at a city bar. Driving himself back in his luxury car, he failed to see the deer in the road along the river. He swerved to the right, too much and careened through the railing down into the rapids below. The cascade killed Son 1 immediately. His car engine ran for hours until it stopped.

Distraught, the father held three memorial services—one for each decade of Son 1's life. He made donations to charities in his son's name. He vowed never to drink a sip of alcohol again. He contemplated suicide.

Son 2 found himself suddenly the recipient of the entirety of his father's attentions. Initially the father wanted to reminisce about Son 1—his accomplishments, his funny mannerisms, his "giving soul." After weeks of photo albums and memories, however, the father shifted to a different mode altogether. He told Son 2 he's like to spend "quality time" with him, to hold onto what's left. Though Son 2 felt like somewhat of a consolation prize, he was also touched by his father's efforts. "I don't want to be a stranger any longer," his father said.

They talked. They went to ball games. They played billiards. They ate Philly cheese steaks. They went to nostalgic reunion-tour rock concerts.

Son 2 thought that the memory of Son 1 would still dominate these bonding efforts—and at first he did. As time passed, the allusions to Son 1's tragedy receded. Son 2 almost began to sense that he *replaced* Son 1. Except he hadn't.

The father's interest waned after about a year. Son 2 was adequate, he supposed. However, ultimately Son 2 was simply lacking in fire and gusto in the opinion of the father. Son 2 was no Son 1.

The father eventually found friends to fill the void of Son 1's death, mostly with friends, cousins, and collectibles. At this point, the father returned to ignoring Son 2.

Son 2, was distraught by the regression. Over time he moved from the area, seldom visiting his parents. The father and mother got divorced shortly before they turned 70. They died within a year of each other, not having spoken to each other or Son 2 in many years.

Ninety-Nine Facts
Concerning My Father

1. My father was a strong man, still is in his own way: he believed in Teddy Roosevelt's dictum about speaking softy; he listened to Sinatra; he wore leather jackets, polished his shoes.
2. At night my father was quite different.
3. This was not known to all.
4. The Oedipus complex has some truth to it; however, what if you don't know your mother? Would Freud say it was still reasonable to possess the secret desire to kill your father?
5. My father was a good businessman—one of the best in Omaha. He sold. Then he sold those who sold. Then he sold those who sold others who sold. It went like that. He didn't simply climb the ladder, by the end he owned the ladder.
6. My father was an expert at commodities trading.
7. He owned more ties than Macy's—or it seemed that way.
8. He was also poor once—in the beginning, when I was a wee nub. When I was a wee nub my mother had enough of him. I can understand the impulse.
9. My father was a weak man.
10. He still is.
11. He couldn't teach a lick. Anything he knew, he hoarded. He kept his knowledge to himself, as if in the mere act of sharing it would lose potency.
12. He seemed to be of the belief that I would learn these things through some process of osmosis.
13. As always he was both right and wrong.
14. My father told me once that he hated lists. "They give you a program, a set series of tasks. If you don't have a list you can do what you're thinking. That's life—doing what you think. Acting on impulse."

15. He wore skirts at night. Most nights. Blouses, hose, high heels, panties, hats. The works.

16. My father would walk around the house in this way. He'd cook in his lady attire, clean up in his lady attire. I wondered if he wanted to be noticed, to be taken care of. This was his means of expressing his desire. His inner being.

17. His skirts had different patterns. When I close my eyes I can imagine them: red and gold and black plaid, hound's-tooth, green and yellow paisley, black and white polka dots.

18. Until I was approximately ten and three months I thought this is just what needed to happen.

19. When I asked my father why my mother left, he said that she thought he was "too rigid."

20. My guess now is that she found out about Earl. Or some proto-Earl.

21. Until I was approximately ten and three months I thought Earl was my father's "best buddy." That's what he called Earl.

22. Earl never taught me how to change a tire either. It was fine.

23. If you asked me what Earl looked like I'd probably ignore your question and stare into my Bloody Mary. If you asked again I'd tell you he looked like Burt Reynolds sans porn-mustache, but more angular.

24. Earl also smelled of mulch. He was a gardener. He always had dirt under his nails. Sometimes the dirt seemed mossy.

25. My father looked like a doughy version of Jeremy Irons, sans the British accent.

26. I'm not personally aggrieved or in therapy or in any ways suffering. I try to avoid forms of thought which lead to self-indulgence, if possible.

27. I read Seneca nightly.

28. I do have a stiff drink or two and find nothing wrong with this. The V-8 in my Bloody Mary offers

plenty of vitamins and minerals. It's a drink that can act as dinner. Sometimes it does.

29. Earl, ironically, was a fan of lists. He thought they promoted clear thinking and a sense of reward once the items on the list are accomplished. He was practical.

30. I found out later that my father would occasionally hire female prostitutes to lie nude next to him at night. He wanted to test his willpower.

31. He hired male prostitutes for that other reason.

32. I am not ashamed.

33. I am ashamed.

34. By age thirty-two my father earned his first million. I was eight. In celebration we ate a cake decorated with green dollar signs.

35. By age thirty-four my father earned his second million.

36. This was the year I discovered Earl and my father in the basement.

37. My father threatened to shoot me if I told anyone. He did not say this calmly. I was already bleeding from the nose at this point. Earl told him to stop. "Just stop already!" Eventually my father did—after my nose was broken.

38. Later my father instructed me that I shouldn't share his secret—for my *own* sake. He instructed me in this, but not spark plugs. He said if the word got out it would "ruin my reputation and yours."

39. He said: "If you think a bloody nose is bad, imagine what kids at school would do to you."

40. I didn't say a thing. I never did. And here I am.

41. I also never invited friends over to my house in fear they would find out.

42. This created suspicion. One friend, Joel, said he thought I was making nukes down there. I joked that I was.

43. I became sullen and withdrawn. At least most of the time.

44. At age ten and eleven months I decided whatever my father did, I'd do the opposite. He was rich—I'd be poor. He was chunky—I'd be rail thin. He was clumsy—I'd be athletic.

45. I joined every youth sports team I could— basketball, football, baseball, hockey, bowling. I lifted weights. I ran.

46. My father told me I was wasting my time.

47. "It makes me happy," I told him.

48. "What makes you happy isn't always in your best interest," he said. "Life doesn't work like that."

49. One night my father was sick in bed. I complained to Earl. Earl was a good listener; calm and patient. Earl told me he'd talk to my father for me. He must have.

50. My father was not trying to punish me because I knew.

51. He punished me for unknown reasons.

52. I can speculate, but does it serve a practical purpose?

53. I grew up, got married, bought a modest home in a city far away from my father.

54. We planted perennials. Irises. Peonies. Hostas for the deep shady parts.

55. We had contractors build a deck.

56. We bought a new stainless steel refrigerator—the kind with double doors.

57. I sent my father occasional sparse e-mails.

58. He rarely, if ever, replied. If he did it would be in all lower-case, lots of typos. He always included the phrase "very busy these days."

59. My wife couldn't stand him. She said he was essentially an absentee father.

60. Earl was long gone at this point—someone else replaced him. My father always liked newer, better.

61. My father, at one point, tried to convert himself. He "found God," or so he said. For a spell.

62. It didn't take.

63. My father told me this later on the phone one night. He was emotional over the loss of his brother (my uncle).

64. It's difficult sometimes to know what's true. There is often an angle.

65. Angles of angles.

66. Five years and four months after moving to the modest home, my father e-mailed to say he would be "in town" for a few days on business. Conference—something of the sort. Could he stay with us? He asked.

67. "Sure," I said. "It will be nice to catch up."

68. I felt insipid just writing it. And masochistic.

69. I knew it was trouble. Some part of me wanted the confrontation.

70. His suit was perfect. His hair was gray, but coiffed. His tie looked immaculate, as if painted on.

71. Perhaps it was the gum he chewed or his aftershave. He smelled citrusy.

72. We put him in the basement guest bedroom. It was pleasing to see him hunkered.

73. He slept for a while. I remember that. He said he was worn out from the flight. This was pleasing, also.

74. We had dinner—the three of us. My father, my wife and me. It was pork chops with spring potatoes and asparagus. He only ate three potatoes. One spear of asparagus. "I don't like peeing stink so much. That is the downside, right?"

75. He said he is "watching his girlish figure."

76. My wife kicked my shin. He was still on the "down low."

77. My father told us a story about hiking in the Canadian Rockies. It wasn't like him to tell stories, or to go hiking. He said he went there two years ago with "a friend." They hiked half-way up some mountain, he said, and when they looked over the

vista they could see glacial lakes—"an otherworldly color," he said. "Something from another planet, almost. It was as if I stepped into one of my dreams."

78. I wasn't sure what the point of his story actually was at first.

79. But then I could visualize it—the aqua-marine lakes, the mountain peaks. My father was—in his own way—attempting to console me. Or comfort me. This is what I thought at least.

80. We all slept.

81. The next evening my wife came home from work to find my father in the living room, drunk out of his mind. There was a puddle of vomit seeping onto/ into our Persian rug. She called me. I sped home.

82. He was unconscious at first. "It's so odd," I said. "My father doesn't drink."

83. "Well, he does now," my wife said.

84. We managed to raise him enough to get him to bed. He made gestures to puke again. What could we do?

85. My wife went upstairs to clean the mess. That vile intestinal smell permeated the room.

86. I sat next to my father on the bed. His eyes looked gummy.

87. "I tried to smother you one night," he said. "You were asleep. Maybe six. I didn't want you. I tried to snuff you out."

88. "I don't remember that," I said. Flat.

89. "That's good. Because it happened."

90. "Why didn't you go through with it then?"

91. "I couldn't accept the punishment—jail, the death penalty, whatever they would give me. If it wasn't for that…"

92. "Oh."

93. "Count your blessings," he said. "The pillow never so much as touched your face."

94. I closed the door. I wanted to lock it, set the room ablaze.

95. I never mentioned what my father said to my wife, to anybody. We have two daughters now—neither has met their grandfather.

96. When my father left the next morning, I wasn't sure if he even remembered his disclosure, anything about the day before at all.

97. He shook my hand. He has a weak handshake. I've always hated that. I wanted to tell him I hire hookers to lie down next to me. Just like he did. For the temptation. But I didn't say a word.

98. That night my wife and I ordered pizza, watched some insipid T.V. movie—to decompress.

99. We fell asleep in front of the television glow, on the couch, legs locked together. We slept like that through the night. It was good. And I didn't dream a thing.

Tanglewood Days

We are united in our hatred of slackness, in our loathing of loose morals. No, "morals" doesn't quite capture the notion—let's call it "understanding."

We are precise.

We live in a house of 2,346 square feet. We have two and a half bathrooms, fifteen windows, three doors. We have eleven chairs—far too many chairs really. (How many chairs do I actually use on a regular basis?) We own three bottles of squeezable hand soap. Two peelers. Six lamps. This is my son and me.

My sweet, mute son. Well, not exactly "mute" exactly. Quiet. Subdued. He just seldom speaks. He is blonde and bug-eyed and dormant—a volcano about to erupt.

We live on an eroding yard overlooking a drainage ditch. The drainage ditch is dry, scabbed with cracked mud as a result of the drought. We are suffering.

I call my ex-wife. She lives one thousand three hundred and ninety-eight miles away. She has renounced her motherhood. "Renounced" is my way of thinking about it at least.

She has removed herself from what she calls the "shackles of society."

This is better than the alternative—a life of quiet desperation.

--Jack. How is Jack doing?

--I'm fine.

She likes to refer to me in the third person—takes the sting out, I suppose. She exhales through her nose volubly.

--Brenda is enjoying the wind here. This is her. She is cultivating. I try to think, not feel.

She's in New Mexico.

--I'm keeping my head together, I say.

--Yes, yes.

--Giles will be five next week.

--Oh, well that is not my obligation. Is it? Kiss his head for me.

--Brenda, I say. Do you listen to yourself? He's not going to know you. You're okay with that?

--Yes, yes. The wind is good here.

This is the way it goes.

I step out onto the deck, look out over the drainage ditch. Brenda refers to it as a water-front property. She has a way of lifting her top lip to expose her teeth. Like an orangutan.

I feel the wind here.

Giles will be home soon. Next year he will be in kindergarten. The solstice is coming. If we were in Alaska it would be light all day and night. I think of this. Canadian geese pluck at the grasses by the muddy water.

Giles is making foam castles. With the money Brenda sends, I buy him one toy a month. This month: foam blocks—like Nerf Legos. I parent by entertainment. I suppose I'm not alone in this. We count the foam blocks first. Both of us.

--It helps to know how many we have, doesn't it?

Giles nods. He's glad to be done with school. I never let Giles draw, however, lest he draw his mother. I have placed sticky notes over her face in all the photos in the house.

We seldom speak. Sometimes she crafts a gnomic letter. It usually takes me days to work up the nerve to read them.

There's Mike. Mike eases the nerves like a glass of Shiraz. Best of all, Giles and Mike get along smashingly. Mike has a well-developed sense of childishness. This helps. They "fish" in the "lake" with twine and plastic worms. Giles tells stories about the fish he saw. He stumbles over his words and stutters with excitement. I can't complain: my son speaks.

On Giles' birthday Mike spends the night. He smells of strawberries and almonds—neither of which are unpleasant.

Brenda calls a week later and I let her ring through to the voice mail.

--Giles, honey. Happy birthday to you, happy birthday to you. I love you, Mommy's little flamingo. And I hope you do, too! Happy birthday, munchkin. I'll see you soon.

I erase the message. I tell Giles we are heading to the park. We eat peanut butter, English muffins and mandarin oranges. Mike drives.

Giles initially wants to climb the purple dinosaur, but we coax him to the whirligig. I hated spinners when I was a child, yet perhaps Giles will be different, stronger than me. Perhaps he will make better choices. We spin it slow. Giles laps it up.

--Daddy, I want to count the trees over there. Can we? And I want to count the birds, too.

--Do you know what a flamingo is?

--No.

--It's a big, pink bird. Do you know where they live?

--No.

--They live in the salty marsh.

--What's a marsh?

--Doesn't matter. Let's go count the trees.

He swings on Mike's arm. We walk into the woods. I want to tell him how flamingos get their color, but I don't.

Why am I so self-involved? Why must I constantly put myself at the forefront of every single thought? What kind of father am I?

It rains in torrents. For fourteen straight days it rains. The orange ditch spills over into Huckleberry

Road. Cars have to slow down to make their way through the impromptu creek.

Dogs howl in the afternoon.

I wear thick socks frequently. Hiking socks.

I take up swimming—first at the local Y, then I install a small lap pool in what was the den. I do laps four times a day. Giles watches. He makes bird calls, eats strips of Swiss cheese.

Mike calls occasionally, when he's not with James. I try to keep Giles involved.

Those are Tanglewood Days. My nomenclature.

Giles resurrects my spirits, without necessarily trying. He tugs on my shirt. He makes diagrams. He recites the alphabet in French. Despite it all, he's a smart kid.

I dream the roof leaks, but it's fine.

I feel as if the house is crumbling.

One dry night we shoot off fireworks. We're a week from the Fourth of July, but it feels good to initiate something.

I go to work, I come home.

Brenda writes a postcard, says she'll be back this summer. She has been saying this ever since she left.

I hide my stash of dirty magazines in the crawl space, tucked behind the Christmas tree.

I would keep a diary, but it would likely be far too boring to recount.

--Look, honey. It's a boy. She sits upright, surrounded by green—sheets, pillows. Her face looks puffy from tears or medication or bloating or all-of-the-above. My son is Giles. He is the size of a cantaloupe, ruddy and burbling.

Brenda is a voracious reader. She could plow through two books a week. She shames me.

My wife is happy; we both are. We have a young infant; we are starting a family. We have a beautiful new home in a beautiful new development, eat well, listen to beautiful music. We drink exquisite wine, make love to the sounds of wind through the bowers. We are lying in bed. A candle flickers on the night stand. I watch the contorting shadows.

--This is everything, she says.

--What is?

--I can feel it becoming. Brenda has always spoken this way—in non-sequiturs. She assumes you can keep up with her thought stream, and if you don't she leaves you in the dust. It used to annoy me, then I found it endearing, then I found it worrisome. "Worrisome" is where I land.

--I'm not sure what you're—

--*This.* It's a growing sensation. I tried to ask her what she was referring to, but she said she just wanted rest, just wanted to sleep for a long time.

I hold her. We hold each other. In the morning she squeezes orange juice. We eat English muffins with homemade jam. On the deck we hold hands in the morning light.

--This. This is heaven, I say.

She stares over the drainage pit. The wind picks up, scudding the muddy water. The weeds on the bank of the drainage pit lash in the gusts.

--It's windy. It's so windy, she says.

I look up at her. Her eyes scan the choppy water. And far beyond it.

Rooted

I'd be lying if I told you my father isn't a good man. He's a *gem*. If you ask me, he's absolutely perfect.

My father has money: he's tall and handsome, he's witty, he's worldly. Ivy League. He has a beautiful wife (my mother), three children who adore him, and most likely a lovely vixen for a mistress (he would never leave my mother; he'd never act in an indiscreet manner; he'd be "classy" about it).

Though he worked for years at a non-profit (serving the blind), now that my father is retired he spends his time volunteering. Soup kitchens. Domestic violence shelters. He reads to the illiterate. He volunteers for pet clinics. He helps out at children's hospitals. He brings food to the elderly (and healthy food at that). He is good.

It's all a bit much, really.

My father mostly occupies himself, however, with farmers' markets. Each Saturday after the farmers' markets wrap up he's the guy who collects all the castoffs and hauls them to various needy families around town. Given the sheer mass of produce he collects, this duty takes him well into Tuesday morning. The pile of produce (and bread from the bakery and sometimes flowers from the local gardener) is so large that it usually necessitates my father make four or five trips to and from the market.

I know all this because I've accompanied him. The produce stays in the garage as it waits for distribution. The house smells like Old McDonald's shed: onions and potatoes and cabbage and carrots and rutabagas and old lettuce and turnips and peppers and wormy corn and squishy tomatoes and bruised melons. Lots of root vegetables especially—they aren't as popular with the peaches and tomatoes crowd (the majority).

The problem only rests with my inadequacy, my sense of inferiority. Faced with a "good" father of such magnitude it's only human nature, I suppose, to feel miniscule and unworthy. This is me.

This is nothing really new, however; I've felt this way my whole life. Inadequate.

However, my own smallness would simply be an academic issue if it weren't for the following two vital facts: (1) As a forty-three year-old man I live with my father (yes, in the clichéd basement bedroom) and (2) like most heterosexual men, I have the occasional interest in members of the opposite sex.

The inevitable reaction of at least some women to my father runs something like this: "He has such a good heart—and you know what? I value that in a man more than anything. You can tell he really cares about people other than himself. That's so rare. It is. It's pretty attractive really. In a selfish society your father is one person who actually is *aware* of others. I admire him so much."

As you might guess, this creates an implicit/immediate compare and contrast situation—a dilemma. Unless I adopt lepers, I can't possibly live up to my father's high moral bearing (so I seem selfish and petty in comparison). On the other hand, if I attempt to give in the way my father does I'm accused of not being "true to myself." Sheila, Cindy, Anna, Cary—they all essentially fell into the same tar pit.

But then Jenna.

Jenna is different. Jenna sees through the problem inherent at the heart of my domestic sphere.

I pick this up in the way she leans away from my father when he becomes all grin and backslap. When he slides into stories about his volunteer gigs, Jenna has to stifle a yawn.

We drive over to a fish n' chips joint—her request. After we eat we're drinking beers, tossing darts. Jenna's tomboyishness may even trump her contrariness. She likes sports and beer and men. She's a guy's gal. She's fun to be with. She's smart. She's good people.

"Why don't you just get your own place?" She flings the dart. 15.

"Can't afford to." I fling mine. Board. "At least not yet."

"I like you," she says. "But your father." She tosses the next one. 20. "He's kind of in the way, you know?"

"Well, I don't know," I say. Outside the 2.

"C'mon."

"Yeah, maybe a bit."

Jenna loops her hair back into a ponytail. She tells me she finds all the volunteering a bit much. She asks me if he's manicy. I tell her the truth—he's always done that sort of thing. Always.

"Who gains from all that? I mean, is it for them or for *him*?"

I don't know what to say. Nobody has put it to me that way before.

"I'll lend you a grand," she says. "Seed money." She lights a cigarette, takes a drag. She gives me one, also.

So I move out. Only ten minutes away into this tiny 60's-era-one-bedroom. The apartment is inexpensive, but boy, it's seen some better days—that's for sure. The dishwasher is olive green and whirrs as if run by a dozen hamsters: the outlets spark. The walls are nicked and lac-quered with black marks. The hardwood floors appear faded and scuffed.

Still, my own place.

Jenna comes over frequently.

I'm paying her back on a monthly basis.

My father calls. He hurt his knee—wrenched it lugging bags of potatoes. He says he'd like for me to help him out with the produce distribution. Great.

"It's just a lot for me to manage with my knee. Get your girlfriend to help you," he says. He's forgotten her name. He calls her "girlfriend." I can't bear to tell him that Jenna would rather get an appendectomy than think of herself in such a way.

"Okay," I say. "I can help on Sunday."

Then I have to work. I'm assistant manager at a sub shop and we're understaffed as is. So for most of Sunday I'm filling his station wagon with fruits and vegetables, unloading them into baskets splayed all over the garage, then doing it all over again. Backbreaking work and we only accomplished half (if that) of the job. I don't know how he does it.

"It's a labor of love," Mom says. Or of masochism, more likely—I'd like to add.

Jenna's over later. We're watching boxing (her choice) and playing cards.

"What's the point of all of it?"

I tell her it helps the homeless. She says they must inspire other people to donate food, that my father cannot be the only one. We're watching two stubbly Honduran guys pummel each other. The guy with the dragon tattoo is winning.

"Why don't the farmers just sell their leftovers somewhere else?" Or take it themselves to a shelter or something?"

"I have no idea," I say. "He's been doing this a long time—there's a system. You know what, I think he just doesn't like to waste food. Honestly, I think it's that simple."

She puffs air through her mouth and shrugs.

The three of us are standing in the middle of a field. I'm watching the tiny white butterflies shimmy from one flower to the next.

"Is this the spot?" my father asks.

"I think so," Jenna says.

"All right," he says. "But I don't see anything."

"I don't either," I say. Despite the wind, it's humid. We're dripping with sweat. My deodorant melts down my side. I have the string. I feel like a water buffalo.

Jenna walks ahead a bit scouring the grasses beneath. She's walking carefully so she doesn't step on it. She tells me to yank on the string again. I do and the weeds shift ten feet off to Jenna's right. That's all I needed to do.

Jenna comes up with it.

It's a weird kite—yellow with various kelp-like tendrils, reminds me of a jellyfish stuck in the Gulf Stream. We lift it back into the moist sky.

My father wraps his hands around his head in delight. I like seeing him waste time.

"You have a nice girlfriend," he says.

"Jenna."

"Right. She's different. Not abrasive exactly. She's just independent."

Jenna says her ears are burning. She tells my father that I'm so much better off living on my own—that it's healthy for me.

"Yes, it was probably time," he says. I'm watching the kite flop around in the heavy air.

"He's his own person," Jenna says. "And maybe someday he'll be as accomplished as you are."

This is a subtle dig, but I'm not sure if my father will see it as such. He winks and scratches his leg.

"I don't know if I'm accomplished really. Just active."

"You like staying busy."

"I do. It keeps me young."

"Young is good," Jenna says. I give the jellyfish more slack.

"Or the perception of it."

"And perception goes a long way."

"It sure does," my father says. "But I'm sixty-seven. Another ten years I might be in the dirt. Who know?"

We listen to the birds.

I smell the skunk cabbage. I want a shower.

"What if you could live for eternity?" Jenna asks. She likes this kind of barroom bullshit question.

"Couldn't do it. The end makes it sweeter. And passing on the baton."

A week later I break it off. With Jenna I can see where this is going—and though she seems healthier for me than the rest, this is probably an illusion. I know it. I'm at the same point as usual, except instead of being in love with my father, she finds him somehow small and limited.

It's still about him. Can't escape it. His fucking presence is still manifest in every Goddamn conversation.

"It's not him," Jenna says. "What are you talking about? I don't care about your father. It's you. You just—you're stuck in a certain mindset. You want to be your own person. Don't talk about it. Be it."

She isn't angry, just frustrated. There's a difference.

By the winter I decide to move back into my parents' basement. I'm sick of making Kraft Mac 'n Cheese and eating alone on my sad futon. I miss the garage filled with bruised green peppers.

"Your father will be delighted having you downstairs," Mom says. "He could always use a hand."

"I know," I say.

I won't quit my day job. I'm back to the quagmire. Fill in whatever clichés you want about change doing a person good and flush that right down life's everlasting shithole toilet.

He planted the seed, also.

I'm rooted here. My feet aren't going anywhere.

Silent Treatment

1.

Mrs. Tartan, my homeroom teacher in seventh grade, used to say that contradiction is the essence of life. I'm paraphrasing, of course. I write the word "paradox" on my right foot each morning. I use a black sharpie, the kind kids use to get autographs from baseball players. I can tell you more about this, if you'd like—paradox, I mean.

2.

My mother tells me, even to this day, that I'm smarter than I look. Deceptive. I suppose this is a compliment. On the flip side, do I look that thick? It's a rhetorical question really.

I've been thinking about this in light of Mr. Edwards, the guy I was telling you about last time. Before...well, you know. We only have so much time.

At that point I was in my overalls phase. I see, honestly, nothing wrong with overalls. Culturally speaking, they get a bad rap—really. All those Dust Bowl and hickster associations. I'd spy Mr. Edwards staring at me from across the street. I could see the curtains shimmy. I knew he probably yanked himself off at night with me in his thoughts. Whatever. He must've had a thing for freckles, since—as you can see—I'm covered in them. Aaron'd call it dirt, and it always pissed me off. But being ten at the time, this is what gave him pleasure. Another central "p word" that makes the world go round. Mrs. Tartan never talked about pleasure, at least not directly.

3.

I wasn't wary, though I was aware. In retrospect...I know, I know.

So, anyway, I took care of the yard. My mother worked too hard, and Aaron was too young. I did the mowing, the trimming, the raking, the pruning. It wasn't as if we had a huge yard, or anything. But it would quickly become overgrown and ratty. If it was up to my mother we'd just let the entire thing go to seed. She cursed my father about it every day.

I was out there one day, raking. We only had three young red maples, so it wasn't too much labor—not really. I was hoping to finish up in an hour.

Mr. Edwards across the street—he had two large oaks. I knew this because the acorns constantly fell, dinging his roof, landing in the gutters. This is relevant.

So, as I was raking, I kept finding both maple leaves and oak leaves intermingled. The long oak fingers. The hardened stars of the maples. At this point I decided, for some reason, to separate them. Mr. Edwards kept his hair skull-short. Very ex-Marine—which he was. His skin was so pale it almost seemed blue. Yes. And most of all he was alone. I couldn't stand his laser-beam eyes.

When I was done raking I had three clumpy black bags. I stretched the mouths of each one open, withdrew all the oak leaves. Each and every one. I dropped them into a barrow, wheeled the leaves across the street, dumped them in the middle of his lawn. He watched me do it. The whole thing.

I righted the barrow and gawked back at him.

"You like Lipton" Mr. Edwards said. He said it with a sense of reverence, as if Lipton was brewed from diamond dust.

"I need to study for my history exam," I said. "Ancient Rome."

"You've got some nubs on you," he said. "And I can say that. Being a kind of surrogate to you."

I didn't know exactly what nubs meant or surrogates. But I knew enough.

4.

My father used to do the yard work. When I was young I'd watch him, you know. He had a riding mower, so it was quick and easy—concentric circles. But then. The absence of him. My mother would bag the clippings.

He sold tractors, remember? He was the top salesman in the state, which made me wonder why we lived in a run-down split-level, or split foyer. What's the difference between the two, anyway? He had a "conference" to attend, supposedly in Boise. We never heard from him again. My mother said the wickedest thing a person could do to another was cease speaking to a loved one. We all need affirmation. We need talk. A sense that someone in the world cares whether you live or die. My mother said her mother would do give her and her sister the silent treatment often—anytime they messed up. The silence was expansive, she said.

And it was again.

5.

The day after the leaf incident I'm out in the yard again, after school. I have the weed-whacker out and I'm leveling the tall ones by the curb, by the mailbox. Our yard always felt so ratty. Mr. Edwards, on the other hand, mowed his three times a week. The grass barely had a chance to grow. He didn't seem to care if it rained. Ritual.

Then he'd sit on his front porch, watch the tube, read the paper, his glasses perched on the bridge of his nose. Drinking his tall glass of Lipton.

As I'm weed-whacking, I can feel his eye s on me. I turn. Mr. Edwards is sitting on the steps of his porch. I started wondering what the inside of his head looked like, what the inside of his house looked like. So it goes.

6.

It was an overcast, foggy day. Why is it on these days that crows emerge to caw? Do you know? Does anybody?

There were crows in his oak trees. They were all watching us.

7.

I floated over there, more than anything else. I can't recall him even asking. I was just there.

"Lipton?"

"Okay," I said.

He opened his screen door and I entered his house. It wasn't what I imagined at all. The living room was decorated in country kitsch, little wreaths and quilty things Norman Rockwell prints, and even a mounted pheasant on the far wall. He had porcelain figurines on a wooden shelf. It was as if his house was once decorated by a woman, but back in the 70's. I never even thought of a Mrs. Edwards.

I watched his steady gait. He walked to the fridge, pulled out a glass of Lipton. It was pre-made. Ice cubes already clinked in it.

"This tea. It's been waiting for you," he said. He handed it to me. The glass felt cold to the touch. My fingers left little imprints of warmness.

8.

I don't remember much. This is why I'm here. Recall. There was the cold glass, then the smell of baked beans. Breath. A clinking sound. Sounds of machinery. Crickets under the house. Numbness in my mouth, as if I were at the dentist's. The next moment of full clarity was that fact that my wrists hurt—both wrists. It felt like rope burn, but not exactly.

Then I was in my bed at home, shivering under my blankets, my body aching. Maybe a fever. My mother came to me, pressed a warm washcloth to my forehead.

At the time I wrote it off as delirium from the illness. But now. I'm not so sure.

What are the results? I'm not so sure of this either.

9.

I look at myself in the mirror straight-on. I think everyone should—honest self-assessment. Farrah Fawcett hair, overalls, no necklace—no jewelry of any sort—freckles, gangly. There I was.

I don't remember a thing.

After school I went back to the weed-whacking. I zapped them all in half an hour, then hung it up for the day—packed the tools in the shed. Mr. Edwards wasn't there—no eyes, no tea, no television on the porch.

I walked over to his house, stood in his small driveway, pealed bark from his tree. I took a piece of thick bark and with it on the sidewalk in front of his house I wrote the word "paradox." I wonder now if he ever saw that.

"It doesn't matter: tell me the story of what I forgot. That's what I need to find out—the rest of it."

The Toaster

I'm reading David Hume at a coffee shop. One of those coffee shops with carefully ripped and ragged thrift shop couches. I'm contemplating eliminating cause and effect—all that. I don't actually like philosophy, but here I am.

She says she's not really there, ironically. She says she truly likes the coffee there. I tell her I don't usually go out of my way to confirm my taste buds one way or another.

She smirks.

Her hair is dyed that purplish henna color, the way the "cool" and "independent" women do. Lots of kitschy berets. She's short and comes off as rather toad-like, to be honest. But she's sexy on some level I'm trying to pinpoint. Something about her mouth, her chin.

I've somehow already stereotyped her as a conceited Baudelaire-reading, Laurie Anderson listening pocket of annoyance.

Somehow this makes me gravitate to her more intensely. Maybe I enjoy being annoyed?

We exchange phone numbers.

At home I notice she drew a picture of a unicorn on the bottom of the scrap of paper. The horn has a particularly phallic appearance.

The second month is always the most difficult. The first is pure exploration; it's new; it's a thrill. The second month I'm fighting off boredom already. I admittedly move fast. We're already living together.

There is a wild animal spark in her eyes, a hyena ready to devour a carcass.

We mostly stay in, order Thai carry-out, listen to her collection of obscure vinyl. She also has a thing for John Cale, which I don't particularly understand. She reads passages to me from George Saunders, Aimee

Bender, Miranda July. She calls them "supercool." I don't say a thing. She says she's a writer, but I never see her write.

She almost always orders the green curry. She says it gives her an adrenal gland buzz.

I begin recording her as she sleeps—her request. Audiotape. Sounds of her exhaling. Her breath whistles.

"Send them to my father," she says.

"Your father?"

"I have my reasons."

She writes the address in black marker on a large pink envelope. There is something garish and off-kilter about this.

I do what she says. I'm not a man with many secrets. I'm an open book.

"Everyone has secrets," she says.

We drink lots of water. At any given time there are seven or eight half full glasses of water around the condo at any given time. It's okay, I'm in-between things. I'm laissez-faire on unconsumed water.

Her elderly neighbors—the Jackobsons—have complained to the condo board about her. They have said she's a no-good druggie. I'm responsible for testifying on her behalf, which is uncomfortable since I don't know her name. I thought I overheard someone on the phone calling her Camilla, but I can't risk being wrong. I tell her my name is John, though it's not.

This is not a relationship based on trust.

I find out through the condo board that her name is not Camilla. It's Karen Bice. I tell them my name is John Allenton.

"I have never seen her ingest drugs," I say. "Unless you count spicy Thai takeout."

She wants to egg the neighbors' front door. Instead, she snatches their Sunday paper.

"I'm Stan Bice," the man says. I'm standing in the doorway in my boxers and Florida Gator's t-shirt. "Karen's father."

I realize then I hadn't shaved in ten plus days. I probably look like a beatnik ne'er-do-well.

He brushes by me. He's taller than I'd imagine for her father.

"Are you Middle Eastern?"

I know it's an idiotic question as soon as it exits my face. I regret it, though I seldom experience regret.

"You're fucking my daughter and you don't even know where her people're from?"

I shrug.

"Isn't that the kind of thing you ask before—"

"It could be. If I were smart."

"I'm Armenian."

"Okay," I say.

"Her great-grandparents were killed in the genocide. Both of them—her mother's side."

I nod.

I ask him if he'd like something to drink. Cold seltzer?

He doesn't respond. He does not look happy to be here.

Her father stays. He won't sleep on the sofa or floor, so he sleeps in the bed with us. He does take sleep medications though—he admits it helps him zonk out.

We do it very slowly, so as to not wake him. We feel it's fairly safe. Once, in the middle of things, he sighed and turned over. It was difficult to remain aroused after this. His back bore a resemblance to a shag carpet.

He says he was moved by the touching audiotapes of his daughter breathing. "It made me feel like a young father again," he says.

He's not a bad man.

We order Thai again, drink water. She reads us pseudo-hip fiction in the vein of Aimee Bender. The story features a talking toaster who is having an affair with a coffee maker. It runs hot for a while then burns out. I'm wondering why a toaster is male. I'd think, given its slots, it would be of the female persuasion. I don't say a thing.

"I wish I could write like that," she says.

"When is the last time you wrote?"

"I don't know—before I met you, I guess."

"Are you a writer?"

"Yes. What kind of question is that?" Her eyes bug out. I can tell, however, that she is 1/3 amused.

"Well?"

"Yes?"

"When do you write?"

""I don't have to. I am a writer. I am always writing up here." She taps her head. I'm the toaster, I realize. Maybe a toaster oven.

Her father says he'd like to tell her a secret.

"Shoot," she says.

We're eating raspberry Pop-Tarts and pineapple juice. The combination tastes of dish soap. It's morning and we're hungry. We're wolfing down the Pop-Tarts despite the chemical aftertaste.

Her father drinks water.

"You're adopted. You're not even half-Armenian. You know we adopted you, when you were two." He says this is why he is here—to tell her about her past. He needed to divulge, to confess.

I expect a blaring melodrama. She licks the raspberry jam off her thumb, eyeballs her father and takes a slug of juice. Shrugs.

"Okay," she says.

"Okay? That is it?"

"What should I say? I don't care. It doesn't affect me. It's fine."

Her father expected something different. So would I.

"Would you like some coffee, John?" she asks, standing to make it.

I want to tell her my real name, since we're in truth-telling mode. I decide I'll wait until later.

Karen's father doesn't say a word about the love-making. And he's the kind of man who would. Karen says she'll be leaving soon, but she doesn't motion to. She glares instead. I begin to regret shacking up with her.

When I came home Karen's father slouches there on my couch, gut spilling out over his boxers, drinking prune juice.

"Hey, cowboy."

I nod.

"Do you like prune juice?"

"I don't know," I say.

"It's very good for your colon, you know. It cleans you all out. It really liberates you. Quite refreshing."

"So I hear."

"So I'm supposed to ask: how was your day?"

"Are you asking?"

"Yeah,   sure."

I snort. I don't feel like detailing the particulars of my lived experience to this man. Given the circumstances, I'm not even sure I'd like to relate the particulars to Karen either.

I shrug.

"I'm tired," I say. "I'm going to lie down."

"The prune juice will be in the fridge," Karen's father says.

I nod, nod, nod.

I close myself in the bedroom and return to David Hume. I read for ten minutes, fall asleep. All that causality.

Her hair is in my face. She's nuzzling into my neck. I sigh. Now I'm awake, unfortunately.

"Can we do something about your father?" She tells me she owes him money, a lot of money. Tens of thousands. They worked out a deal where he could stay with her indefinitely. He wants more "intimacy" in their relationship. When I press her on this, she tells me he just always wanted to be closer to his daughter. Who doesn't? We all like daughters.

"Is he really your father?"

"What kind of question is that? Yes, of course he is."

Her breath smells of prune juice. This is not promising.

At dinner Karen and her father sit on one side of the table. I sit on the other. They talk about Jim Jarmusch and evangelicals and Sonic Youth. I listen. They talk about cooking and wine and aperitifs and architecture of the 1930's. I listen and feel ignorant.

I masticate. I listen to the sounds of my mastication.

As I watch them I do a little facial compare and contrast—ears, nose, chin, eyebrows, eyes. I don't see a single resemblance between Karen and Stan. This doesn't mean everything, but it means something.

"You like Mystery Train?" Stan asks me. "It's the Elvis one."

I shrug. I'm not an Elvis guy. I have no idea what they are talking about.

I can't bring myself to kick her father out and I can't simply break up with Karen (and kick her out). Instead, I go for a walk. I stroll down Sullivan Street. I pass the warehouses and thrift shops and crystal/pseudo-hippie head shops. I kick at pebbles and bits of broken glass on the median strip and gaze up into the greenish/yellow-tinged polluted air.

My air is polluted too.

When I was six my father used to take me to a small state park in the hills. We'd hike in silence and afterward he'd ask me what my favorite part of the hike was. He wanted the analysis. I rarely had a quality response. I'd usually say, "It was all fun," or something of this sort. He'd try to tease out some particulars from me at the snowball stand. The ice was so cold I could barely open my mouth.

I still can't.

The question is why did he care what I thought?

I don't have so much to add.

When I return I tell Karen I'm moving. I tell her I still like her fine and everything, but that I don't see myself dating her father. This seems intuitive to me. She's eating a plum. What's with all the prunes and plums?

"Okay, well," she says. "Let's just see what happens."

"No, you don't get it; I'm moving," I say.

Her father scratches his hairy shoulder and stifles a burp. He's watching a porno in the corner on his I-Pad. A threesome with two guys going at it with some poor waify Filipino woman with a nose ring. Karen says something, in Armenian, I believe. I didn't know she knew any. Shows how deeply I know her.

She leans over kisses him on the lips, whispering, smiling through her teeth. I can see her tongue flicker between her teeth, slightly. She kisses her father on the head, her "adopted father," whatever he is. Whoever he is. I'm supposed to be envious.

"My father says he'll pay you five hundred bucks a month to stay," Karen says.

I sigh the sigh of the damned. I look away for a long time. I shrug the shrug of the living.

Scraps

My father is a child. My father is a boy of a man.

I'm walking on cracks. I'm walking on sand and grit, broken glass.

He is here; he is somewhere.

The humidity drains me. I sweat buckets. I call the phone number listed on my scrap of paper and I walk.

I walk through villages and towns, past cotton fields and soybeans and chicken farms. I walk through pine forests echoing with the sounds of woodpeckers.

In one of these houses he sits, mopping his sweaty brow. In one of these huts he hunches over the kitchen sink, puking up his guts. Unshaven and foul.

My father the ex-athlete. My father the money man. My father the recluse.

I see him when he allows me. It is a one-way street, a stiff arm.

As I walk I imagine Spartans on the battlefield. Blood for respect, for pride. Father may like me.

I don't know if he's in this state, in this county. I have no idea.

My last contact was four years ago. He was on a live celebrity program. One of these with obstacle courses and dueling mascots and light banter. I called the station.

"I forgot your birthday, didn't I?"

Someone called his name in the background.

"I have to go," he said.

I walk through valleys of wildflowers and butter-flies. I walk past herds of sheep, grazing on hillsides.

I eat cheese and nuts and apples and sawdust crack-ers. I sleep under a towel draped over a birch bower. I walk on in the early morning dew.

I walk past mansions, through neighborhoods of estates, manors. He is inside one of these, somewhere, making love to some woman, sleeping, watching a horror film in his own private theater.

I take it back: he's not a celebrity. He's just a man. I don't know. I never made the phone call. I can't be trusted. But then neither can he.

Maybe he's dead, maybe in Paraguay. Maybe he's a hobo on some freight train rolling North through the Appalachians.

In the desert I shuffle; I admittedly slump. My energy dissipates. I fear my time is ending. The shadows grow longer.

But by the time I reach the cooler foothills I've survived the worst. I am rejuvenated. I breathe deeply through my nose and I can feel the water in my nostrils.

I camp by the creek and eat Spaghetti-O's mixed with a can of white beans. The wind picks up through the spruce knobs. I sleep well.

In the morning I try the phone number on the scrap of paper. I don't receive an answer. No way to leave a message.

I walk on.

I walk into the foothills and rest at the base of the mountains. The mountains are taller than I'd like, than I'd expect.

I don't remember a thing about my father—this is the point of my perplexity. I'm not sure what he looks like exactly. The blur is different to assess.

My mother reminds me with photographs—yet I was so young then. So was he. The colors have faded. His postcards are in tatters. I can't remember what he smells of.

My father is a boy. He can't be a man. He can't be a man if he won't pony-up. He won't pony-up because he is diluted. He is diluted because he lacks the hearth of family.

Once I reach the low-oxygen pinnacle, I can peer down on it all—the foothills and valleys and desert and towns. The cities glimmer by the shore in the far distance.

If I shout loud enough perhaps he will hear me. I'm not sure if I want him to. In some ways I'm better off hung-up, breathing his thin air—looking out over it all. Perhaps he needs me invisibly searching.

Corresponding

The angel on top.

I drink warm milk from a bowl, writing to my father.

We correspond bi-weekly, like two forlorn relatives from some dusty Victorian novel.

He had forty-five angels, which he would rotate on a tri-annual basis.

I wear thick socks and hiking boots.

I'm writing about the water irises I plant by the lake.

I'm responding to his queries regarding my poetry; I tell him I'm in a morass (four days straight working on one line).

I'm anti-competition, not anti-social.

My students used to refer to me as witchy, though it wasn't meant to be derogatory.

I'd rather walk around my flat nude, if it's all the same to everyone; this sixty-three-year-old body holds up.

He was so obsessed with Christmas he had four trees.

I am not superficial.

I'm writingwritingwriting, but I'd love to take a nap.

I do need my daily swim, also.

My pen is writing to him, though my mind strays afield.

This is okay—it's all family.

I was born in a widow's caul—this does not mean my father is defective.

A week later I'm reading his letter.

He's postulating.

He's speculating.

In person, my father is unassuming, but in writing he's charismatic.

Charisma is an under-appreciated quality.

I'm eating my favorite meal—a cold egg sandwich, with a tomato slice or two.

I have robbed a grave once.

I used to keep guinea pigs in a hollowed-out television frame on the back deck.

My right eye is blind from staring at a solar eclipse.

My father says my "lake" isn't really a lake—that I need to "gain some perspective before it passes me by."

He says my lake is a lack.

I am formulating my response as I chew my egg salad.

I have written forty-six poems since last week.

This is not that many for me—I once wrote ninety-eight in four days.

It would take my father weeks to decorate for Christmas.

My father says my lake is really just "a drainage ditch."

Being born in the caul makes me a better person.

Perhaps this has something to do with my affinity for thick socks, and my fear of exposing them.

My heart rarely aches.

My father tells me I need to "get laid."

This is not rare.

I will send out my poems—many poems.

Someday—one day—someone will remember me for my ninety-eight volumes of poetry.

If I fail to catalogue my experience it doesn't exist.

I will walk around the lake and kick pebbles and dried twigs into it.

This is what one does at the lake.

Say what you will to undermine me.

I'm doing it anyway.

The Door

1. My father's door is locked and I don't have the key. The door appears different than it used to, also—I suspect he upgraded. Now it looks like a thick, oak door—painted a dark maroon, the color of dried blood. I don't remember it this way. Affixed to the door: a black knocker reminiscent of a dungeon. The ring is heavy and when I let it drop, it feels as if it might take out a chunk of the door. I stand there for ten minutes, peering in the small rectangular windows by the door. Bleary. Nothing. The sky is heavy with rain and the winds tick up. This is no small matter.

It has been a long time since I have seen him, and my brothers cautioned me against it. But I must—this is not a question. I must know. And I have enough youthful energy to wait him out.

The neighbors across the street are watching me, so I slink down the sidewalk and to the park and down the mulchy path that leads down to the river. It is the afternoon but I wish I had a flashlight or my phone—it is so dark. The gnats are thick and heavy and I can hear the insistent whine of insects in the blooming rhododendron and mulberry trees. Nuthatches squeak from the bowers. I smell the loamy soil and the scent of dead matter and decaying leaves. I would like to curl up under a tree in a dark and hidden space and sleep for two days. I do not. I keep moving and try to forget what happened.

When I reach the river I walk along the bank. Mosquitoes feast on me and now I'm itching and sweating both. Welts appear on my arms. I have no idea what I'm doing down here. The river runs slowly and even when I stop walking and just sit by the water, I can't hear a thing. Not even a whisper. Frogs begin to croak from the swampy areas off to the right. I never mind hearing frogs, especially this early in the year—not even them. I think about jumping in the water to swim with them. Instead, I watch shadows loom and I fall into a daydream.

2. My father's door is locked and I tap on it several times, using the tips of my fingers. Just like last time, I see cars in the driveway and movement behind the drawn curtains, but nobody answers and it's impossible for me to get a bead on the events happening around me.

"Is there something I can help you with?" A man with a head like a cantaloupe squints at me. He wears a clam-digger hat and tiny sunglasses and zinc oxide is smeared on his nose and chin and cheeks.

I tell him and he says I better try again later because my father is not at home and in this neighborhood there is a patrol car that swings by every half an hour, and they do have the power to call the police, and they are armed.

"This is my father's house," I say.

"Or so you say," he says. I can't read his eyes behind his glasses for any trace of sarcasm. But I don't hear any in his voice.

I leave my car parked by the curb and walk back to the main road and along it. SUVs and cars rattle by and someone throws a plastic 7-Up bottle at me—it skids along the road in front of me, sizzling into the dusty reeds. Black and orange beetles cluster in the road grime, feeding on something unseen. Crows gather along the telephone lines.

I duck into a cafe to escape the sun. The woman behind the counter points to the chalk boards behind her—which list sandwiches, soups, salads. I am not hungry. I just want tap water, but I know I need to buy something and I barely have the money for it. I end up buying a coffee and a fruit cup. The fruit is cold and the sugar hits the spot. The coffee, however, tastes a bit sour, but I'm alert after drinking it, so it was essential.

There is nobody else in the shop.

I begin talking to the woman, who has a kind face and who seems, for some unknown reason, petrified.

"Do you ever have the feeling that everything is about to collapse? It's like this sense of dread that I get all the time," she says. "Even though, as far as I know, everything is fine. I'm probably just reading too many news reports."

I tell her that I don't think about that. I only have enough time and energy to think about myself and my family. I guess I'm lazy in that way.

"That's a great way to conserve energy," she says. This time, I can see her eyes—and I do not believe she is jerking my chain.

It is hot as blazes. I never want to leave this place. I love this woman. Who is she?

3. I try again, but his door is still locked and I knock a hundred thousand times and call the number I have for him (not sure if it is even still valid). He just lets the phone ring and ring. I have no idea what I'm doing here any longer. I feel as if I'm repeating the same life mistake over and over again and yet I really can't help it—I feel old and my joints hurt.

The door appears weather-beaten and the stain peels in places.

His car is not in the driveway and I see zero signs of life from inside.

Maybe I should simply come back another time. It seems as though my car is almost out of juice. It was difficult even turning the engine to get it to drive here.

Nobody is watching me, so I enter the back gate his backyard. Peering up into the windows around the back of the house does not give me a greater sense of optimism. The overgrown grass juts out at unlikely angles. Birds lift themselves from the grass as I walk through it. I can hear mice and other small animals rustle unseen.

The yard smells of October somehow. The sky is high and blue.

I expected his yard to be more foreboding or forlorn but it is rather nondescript, save for the pink and green garden gnome and the moldy birdfeeder. I tap on the head of the garden gnome and it sounds hollow inside. I wonder if my father stores anything in there. But when I attempt to lift the garden gnome, it is far too heavy. This is an oddity. I pee behind the shed, against the fence there that protects me (I hope my urine erodes the wood somehow).

I sit in the black iron chair in the shade and fall asleep. When I wake up night has fallen.

I don't bother attempting to call my father. It seems hopeless.

I may die not knowing.

4. My fingers lack the strength to lift the knocker or knock. I look for a buzzer but I don't remember one here. The cold is not a problem, but I'd rather be inside looking out at it than being outside looking in. I stand there blowing on my hands, hoping he spots me from inside and calls me in and offers me a warm beverage to drink as we embrace and chat about the good times and reminisce. However, these are pure fantasies. The reality seems to be that I lack a father. Any real semblance of one, at least. I glance at my pictures of him on my phone and wonder how long it has been. Perhaps my brothers have had better luck—I should ask them.

I walk in the opposite direction, directly into the sun. My sunglasses help but the low sun and glare make it impossible to see and I constantly run into parked cars and mail boxes and the curb. I have no idea where I'm going, just passing houses and cars and mailboxes, cars and houses and mailboxes, mailboxes and cars and houses. I notice the colors repeat themselves, also-- taupe and navy blue and this reddish brown and black and gray and then back to taupe. It's a nice neighborhood, though I can't see a single person outside. I see smoke emerging from chimneys and I see lamps and movement behind curtains and one man in a blue sweater drives up ahead of me and parks along the street, emerges from the car, jangles his keys and walks up the drive to his house.

I'll never tell anyone what happened.

I'll never tell a single person.

I just hoped to talk to my father about it--he was the only person who knew and who I could rely upon. But the power of expulsion. But the sophisticated method of non-disclosure. Ethical hijinks. Nobody wanted to revisit the past if they didn't have to. Live for today, brush everything else under.

As I continue walking I realize that I might never escape this place. I see the same house that I walked by twenty minutes ago--it has to be. Either I'm really walking in a circle or I'm in some kind of loop. Or everything just looks identical to me now. My thoughts are squirrelly and not to be trusted. It's a miasma.

Someday I will just drop dead in the middle of one of these walks, thinking of what I might say to my father. A child with a dog will come across me and his dog will chew on my hand until it bleeds and the child will smack the dog with the palm of his hand and tell him how grateful he is that they are together. Even though I'm dead, I will still process some of this, as if by molecular osmosis. It will stick with me as I melt into the ground, as the beetles and worms and other small animals ingest me and break me down into something that is no longer there.

Jubilation

I washed my face and someone took my spot.
Someone was pleading with me to come back. Yeah, I
gave in and told my father all about it: the chanted
singing in the courts, the constant humming and
whistling, the nah-nah-nah intonations. Let's put it this
way: he was not amused, not a whit. I still have no idea
what tipped me over the precipice. What compelled me
to spill the beans? "Cecilia" popped up one too many
times on Pandora—maybe that's it. That infuriating
song.

He thrummed his thumb on his knee. His class ring
lent extra weight. It was not a musical sound. It was the
sound of rectifying wrongs, the pensive drumming of
plans. As pater familias, he had duties far beyond the
purchasing of bacon. Protection and retribution—those
were within his purview also. As I saw it. The rumpus
room in the basement filled with shiny dangerous things.
Kept under lock and key. Maybe I knew that by telling
him something would happen. I could fantasize but by
telling him they transmorphed into reality.

As a little girl I had no idea what jubilation meant.
And why was I crushing his heart? No clue—I was eight.
I thought they were napping on the mattress in the after-
noon—what else could they be doing?

I detailed my aggravation and innocence and frank
confusion and he listened—all these years later.

"Cecilia, I know what I will do," he said. I glanced
at his fingernails. It appeared they had not been cleaned
in a year, and ragged edged at that. His ovoid belt buckle
caught the fire light. It looked like a bullet, a squashed
animal. The cherry hissed and the hickory popped.

"I *know* what to do," he almost rumbled.

It was an era of kickball and tetherball and racquet-ball and volleyball and four square. Red dimpled balls that required blowing up, squeezing to see if they contained enough air. Me a little pipsqueak roustabout with pigtails and crooked teeth in the court complex, squash courts, racquetball courts. Each court was its own room—with its streaked walls and blue and red lines and polished wooden slats. This was long before the car accident and mother slamming my hand in the door and the long slog through tortuous school repetition. My eyes hadn't yet gone crisscrossed from memorizing names of rivers and the periodic table and dates of wars from the 17th century. I was there for my own amusement. I volunteered to attend this tomboy sports camp—unlike the many others later which I was compelled to join. When I saw the advertisement in the paper insert I knew: the squinty little picture of the boy, his hands lifted in the air as he ran and smiled into the beam of sunshine: I wanted to bolt around like him. I wanted to be him, to know that I to could live with such liberation, such carelessness.

And on the first day it was Greek dodge and getting pegged in the back with a sidearm hurl. Stung like a nest of wasps. And I was happy that way. I could keep up with the eleven year-old boys, no problem. Mr. Preston saw me from above and clapped. "You show them, little feets," he said. "Nobody can rip you away from you." I didn't know what to make of any of it, really. He had hair down to his shoulders like a girl and it curlicued in sweaty waves. His eyebrows arched and his chin protruded like the nose of some ancient ship. He wore sunglasses at all times, indoors and out. When I looked at him I saw only my own reflection.

I hurled the ball and just missed the tall, gangly girl—the one with the braces and the limping left foot. Go for the injured. Take their legs out if you have to, I thought. I was a mean-spirited elfin turd.

After lunch it was Mr. Preston again—this time on his court (number eight in the corner) where we did suicide sprints for ten minutes then reflex drills with browned tennis balls. Good for our spirits, he said. This was the All or Nothing Class, he said. We would do a variety pack and with only twelve of us, he could march us this way and that until our parents drove to snatch us away from the jaws of defeat.

On the third day Mr. Preston started humming. I had the very same exact name as the girl in the song, he said. He called it low hanging fruit. Later I realized I didn't like thinking of myself as something to be consumed. It was an oldie that his parents had on a vinyl record in the basement. He had to intone it, he said. Virtually no choice in the matter—same name!

Nah-nah-nah. Nah-nah-nah-nah. Nah-nah-nah-nah-naaaaaah.

Nah-nah-nah. Nah-nah-nah-nah. Nah-nah-nah-nah-naaaaaah.

Nah-nah-nah. Nah-nah-nah-nah. Nah-nah-nah-nah-naaaaaah.

I can still sing the song by heart, each awful, mocking note. Confidence shook. Knees rattled. Rolling on the floor laughing. He followed me around court eight belting it out for all to hear. I could feel their eyes trace up and down.

It was torture. It was jubilation—for them at least.

All the while Mr. Preston chortled, pointing at me as if I was accused of some awful crime. As if I deserved it.

I took it for three days nodding along or plugging my ears, but on the fourth even my eight-year-old self couldn't take it for one more minute. We were working on badminton. Boys against girls. The little birdie flying up into the wall of the court and then cascading down, as if injured. I thwatted it hard, but into the net.

97

Nah-nah-nah.   Nah-nah-nah-nah.   Nah-nah-nah-nah-naaaaaah.

Nah-nah-nah.   Nah-nah-nah-nah.   Nah-nah-nah-nah-naaaaaah.

It bored in my head, grated. Even with my fingers in my ears it leaked through.

"Mr. Preston," I said. "Why are you doing this to me?"

This is what snagged him. He had no answer. The other campers looked at him. We all waited for a reply. After some time he said, "Proceed with the game."

I told nobody. But that Friday morning I cried in the car.

My father drove me, on the way to work.

"I don't know—I'm just thinking of a sad story," I said. It was too ridiculous to admit.

"Are you sure?"

He patted my knee. It would be okay.

I nodded and I said nothing.

But it stuck with me—I did not forget.

My mother apologized for the hand incident (she slammed the door in anger and had no idea I was right there, she said—I half-believed her). She acted out in frustration too often, she later confessed. She was not frustrated with us—it was her husband.

My father and mother divorced when I was twenty and living away from home. My younger brother suffered the worst of that.

I grew up and graduated from an all girl's college, where I felt suffocated and thinned by the lack of sexual conflict. I never did meet a guy and felt then and later that I had trouble relating.

At twenty-seven I began researching Mr. Preston. I discovered that he became the principal of a high school as well as the assistant football coach. He bought his house for nearly a million. He was married to a woman, older than him, who was a partner in a famous law firm (most notably she represented the guy who was accused of slaying his parents over an argument in a Denny's Restaurant). He drove a black 2019 BMW convertible and owned two dogs, both striking Dalmatians.

All of this I handed over to my father. For years I had forgotten, mostly, until my best friend Sheila reminded me in an e-mail—whatever happened to that hippie camp counselor? The one who had a crush on you?

"He did *no*t have a crush on me," I said. And I believe that. It was purely a case of pushing me around for no reason.

I am not sure why I told my father. It made no sense to me because I knew that he would lash out. On some level I wanted Mr. Preston to suffer. My father, also.

What are you going to do? I asked him. And he told me, frankly.

You can't do that, I said. Not only because there will be consequences but because it is over-the-top. Nobody deserved that. Especially not for singing a Simon and Garfunkel song. Even one about making love to an eight-year-old.

But I knew where Mr. Preston lived and I gave him the address despite myself. Knowing what might happen. Knowing that if he still had long floppy hair and the voice of a turtle dove he might find himself *unde*r the house by the end of the night.

It was a balmy July night, the kind when it seems the sun would never descend. Its glow lingered in the sky hours until ten, eleven, twelve. I *had* to follow my father. I had no choice. The road was straight for the most part, with a ton of lights—so I had to hover back and hope I could stay on green. Luckily my father drove slow (maybe in an attempt to mask his anger). As we got within five miles of Mr. Preston's house, I called the blue line. 9-1-1, easy enough. No way I would let him go through with it. You ask me, small price to pay—the sacrifice.

I'm positive my father knew—even though he never saw me. Ended up being six months (lucky it wasn't more), and when he got out he was an improved man, even he said so. He walked firmly. He stood with both feet on the ground. He rarely slouched. Changed man, my father said. He sold his guns and his knives and began going to group therapy. He met my mother at the mall and they sat on a bench and he got down on his knees for three seconds and clasped her to him.

He still thrumped his jeans with his fingers and that concerned me. But only when watching the game. All that tension, he said. His hair had gone gray, and he napped often. Something inside me clicked.

There was one old pocket knife left I found in the garage behind some rusted out paint cans. Green and yellow and the steel shone in the florescence. I slipped it in my pocket and into my desk drawer. I was almost thirty, I realized, and still living with my father like some kind of refugee from another era. I turned the knife in and out of my fingers all night, sleeping an hour and then waking to pace around my room and into the kitchen. I liked the weight of it in my palm, its coolness.

Later that week I drove the same path my father took. But I took it fast, so I couldn't change my mind. He would hear my side of things, I knew. My truth, as it were. I drove really fast and ran a few lights, I won't lie. His car was right there in the driveway, too. Dull and gray like Mr. Preston's stupid face.

Nah-nah-nah. Nah-nah-nah-nah. Nah-nah-nah-nah-naaaaaah.

Did I hesitate? I had the chance to back down. But

I didn't. Washing my face, huh? What are you begging for now? Is your confidence shaken?

Jubilation, I thought. Jubilation.

Acknowledgements

"The Toaster" was published by *Hotel Amerika*.

"The Invisible Hand" was published by *Boulevard*.

"Baby Carrots in Two Hundred and Forty-Four" was published by *Penduline Press*.

"99 Facts Concerning My Father" was published by *Crab Fat Literary Magazine*.

"Tanglewood Days" was published by *Apalachee Review*.

"Rooted" was published by *Fredericksburg Literary and Arts Review*.